CW01266248

THE PUNK

First published in 1977
by Polytantric Press

Sleeve Design by Graham Bendel and Tina Vaughan.

Large thanks to Craig Sams for all his help. And to Tina for introducing the book to me, and Bruce for font counselling.

Printed by Chapman Graphics.

written by Gideon Sams

Published by Fortune Teller Press

1. The Roxy.

It was Saturday night. Adolph was standing on Shaftesbury Avenue. He had been there for about ten minutes waiting for his friends. Adolph stared at the crowd to see if they were there. They weren't, but Adolph saw some Teds walking down the street. They were quite old, in their late twenties. They were with their girl friends, and were obviously drunk. Adolph couldn't see anywhere he could hide. It was too late, one of the Teds had spotted him.

"Ere look! It's a bloody punk, let's stick a safety pin in his gut."

The other Teds laughed and one or two of the girls laughed as well. Adolph noticed one, a very beautiful looking girl who was standing next to a very big, and very tough looking Ted. The girl looked as if she was almost apologetic about the situation. She pulled her boyfriend back, he was so drunk he turned around and was about to hit her when she cried out,

"No Ned, please leave him, he's done nothing to you. Besides if you get nicked by Old Bill again you'll be in Wormwood Scrubs before you can say, 'Where's my Brylcream?' and I don't want to have to wait for you to get out."

The Ted frowned. Her argument obviously made some sense to him. He moaned,

"Okay, it's a couple of weeks since I beat up a bloody punk, an' I don't want 'im to think he's gonna get away wiv nothing, but if yer don't want me to kick his head in I won't."

The other Teds moaned, but a reproachful look from the big one's girlfriend shut them up. The big Ted was obviously in charge, the girl thanked the Ted and kissed him on the cheek. The other Teds jeered at him but he turned around with a menacing look on his face and all fell silent.

Adolph looked at the girl again. She was quite tall for a girl and had black hair which was cut and styled in a sort of late fifties early sixties shape. She was wearing a white cotton cardigan with two tiny blue stripes on each cuff, and a large 'T' in red letters. Underneath the cardigan she was wearing a low-cut flowery dress with white shoulder straps and hem. The pattern looked nice and went with her face, which was a slightly tanned colour; she looked sort of Gypsyish with her dark skin and deep red lips. Her legs were as brown as her face and were perfectly formed. They were neither fat nor thin, and looked very smooth and beautiful in her bobbie socks, which barely covered her ankles. The girl's shoes were much more modest and in fact were only an expensive pair of sneakers with a yellow stripe set against the pink colouring of the leather.

At this moment Adolph's friends came over. They were four particularly vicious looking punks; Sid Sick, Bill Migraine, Johnny Vomit and Vince Violence. None of these names were their born names, but punks like to have odd, and often depressing names, as is their nature.

The five punks set off for the Roxy, a punk rock venue situated in Covent Garden. When they got there, they joined the large queue of fantastically dressed people. Each person tried to be more disgusting or weird then the next. There were many fights and scuffles in the queue, although none were serious. One of the favourite pastimes of Adolph and his friends were insulting the straight people who walked past the queue, although that wasn't half as much fun as jeering at the rich and famous personalities who walked past the queue to check their names on the guest list. Adolph hated these people who seemed to him to be nothing more than a bunch of posers and 'plastic' people. Adolph despised the rock stars and groups, such as The Who and Led Zeppelin. They talked about fighting the system and capitalism but always ended up as rich as millionaires, giving away back stage passes to the Queen and Elizabeth Taylor.

At last the queue was jammed into the very bare room that had virtually no breathing space. A band was playing at the time and Adolph pushed through the sweating, pogo dancing crowd until he was near the amps because the noise was almost unbearable. Some kids next to him were kicking each other. One of them smashed a bottle against the stage and chucked it into the crowd as a warning gesture to anyone who thought they might help the other punk. Then the kid lunged forward hitting his opponent in the stomach with a head butt.

The other kid grabbed the punk's safety pin earring and pulled it from his ear. Blood gushed out at a surprisingly fast rate. The boy's earring had ripped a large chunk from his ear, which also appeared to be hanging very loosely from his head. The boy had fainted, and was now lying in a small pool of blood around his head. The other punks ignored the whole scene and kept on bouncing up and down, waving their arms around and pushing others away, as if in an endless battle to keep a small slice of territory for personal use.

The music stopped and Adolph looked around. The first group had finished and were now hurling abuse and beer cans at the packed audience, who, by all appearances, didn't seem to think that the Dead Dogs had done a very good set. There was a lot of shouting and gradually a chant began, "Sick! Sick!", the crowd shouted.

After five minutes, they got annoyed and started to hurl beer cans and paper cups at the stage, where a few nasty looking punks were setting up some instruments. Presently the band was ready and the crowd roared, but above the crashing lead guitar and frantic drums, there was a song:-

"Gimme death
don't want life
just gimme death
or I'll kill your wife
had enough of the social security
had enough of life
I want death
yeah I want death
just gimme death
or I'll kick you in the head
then you'll be dead
I'll chop you up
give yer to my cat
because I need death!"

The singer, Johnny Blood, picked up a cup of beer and threw it into the frantic audience, who were jumping as high as they could, trying to punch holes in the battered ceiling of the club. The band continued, playing a set of about fifteen songs, which is a lot for a Punk band. At last the audience was let down from the cloud they'd been sitting on, a highly explosive cloud, with a sweaty, electric atmosphere you could get a shock off.

Soon the gig was over, and a tired but happy crowd of Punks poured from the battered Roxy and descended upon the fearful street. Adolph wandered home with his friends, who were in a jubilant mood after the gig. Adolph shared their feelings, but deep down he felt something else too. He was wondering where the Teddy's girlfriend was.

2. Adolph.

Adolph Sphitz walked along the long corridor on the twenty-first floor of Trellick Towers, a massive tower block overlooking North Kensington and the Westway. The lights of the Westway sprawled out towards the city, like a giant snake curling along between the desolate wastelands and the dilapidated houses. There were no cars on the motorway now. The streets were dark. The city slept in the early hours of the morning. As Adolph walked the wind made a faint howling noise as it swept between the cracks and crannies in the buildings.

Although only a few years old, Trellick Towers had become a grim place. The architects who designed it had not used much imagination. The flats were like small parcels arranged along the corridor. It was up to the flat dwellers to try and make their flats real homes, but not too many people had the colour or vitality in their life to bother.

At last Adolph came to the door of his flat. His mother was asleep, his father was on the night shift at the local police station. Adolph knew that his father hated punks, as well as all other young people. When Adolph changed his name from David, his father tried to throw him out, but Adolph's mother was so upset she almost had a breakdown and his father had to call him back. Adolph didn't like living with them but he had neither money or a job, so he had to stay where he was for now.

Adolph unlocked the door and walked quietly to his bedroom. He went straight to his old, beaten up record player. He lifted the lid and placed the needle on the record. Almost immediately a blistering noise of guitars roared from the speakers in each corner of his room. It was 'Death' the new single from 'Sick'. It was just a repeat of one or two riffs and lasted for about three minutes. All of a sudden the record stopped. Adolph placed the needle back in its place and sat on his bed.

He rearranged his tangled hair back to its original spikyness and removed the safety pins from his nose and ears. Adolph was ready for bed.

3. The employment exchange.

Adolph woke late. He turned over on his side and looked at the clock on a small table beside his bed. On the left was a window that looked out on the houses below. Up in the clouds, high up in Trellick Towers, Adolph felt that he was looking down on reality. He was just an observer, but not actually a part of the life of the flats. The clock said 12.30. Adolph looked at the sky. It was another dark, cloudy day. It looked like rain. Adolph had lost count of the days since there'd been some sun. The weather outlook was a reflection of Adolph's mind, which had been severely troubled for some time. Adolph felt empty and even lost for the last few months.
Adolph dragged himself out of bed and pulled on a battered pair of jeans that had lain crumpled in a

heap upon the floor. He buckled up the heavy leather belt he always wore and put on a black shirt that had been wrapped round a chair nearby. He did up the buttons, leaving three undone at the top. Adolph put on a clean pair of socks and slipped his feet into some Dunlop sneakers. He stood up and walked over to a small dresser that was situated in the corner of the room. He slipped an earring into his left ear. It was a gold swastika surrounded by the star of David, painted in sky blue. Adolph stuck a safety pin in a hole in his nose, then with a final sweep of his arm he brushed his hand through his hair so that it stood up in a mess on his head.

Soon Adolph was sitting at the kitchen table. He read a paper and ignored his mother, who was standing around bashing pots and pans.

"I don't see why you can't be like any other boy. Your father never wasted his studying time running around trying to be different. Why don't you go and get that job which they offered you at the Employment Exchange? What's wrong with cleaning lavatories?"

"I don't like cleaning up shit! That's why:" shouted Adolph.

"I won't have any filth in this house;" barked his mother, then her face went drawn and old and she burst into tears.

"You're our only child, son. Come on why don't you do something to make us proud of you. Your father always wanted you to become a policeman, even walk on the same beat as him." She stopped and sobbed tearfully, "but you had to have it your way, and be someone different."

Adolph had had enough of this. He slammed the paper down onto the formica top of the table. The weak table vibrated and a fork clattered to the floor.

"Why don't you just shut your face! When I want to hear your pitiful sob stories I'll ask for them!"

With this he shoved his chair away from the table, got up, and stormed out. His tea was left standing on the table. (He had already been wearing his pink plastic jacket and had a form for the Employment Exchange).

By now the sky had clouded over and the bleak grey forms threatened rain. It was cold and depressing; Adolph shivered. There was a queue of ten or so people outside the entrance door to the Exchange. A bureaucratic looking man checked his watch and looked to see if everyone was at their posts. He took a pride in his job and never started too early or too late. Finally he stood up straight and striding forward with an air of dignity, he unhooked a rope across the door and let the queue in. The people walked forward and quickly found places opposite stern looking people who had small files on the desks between the walls of booths. Adolph shuffled up to a booth and sat down in an uncomfortable chair.

A stern looking woman sat on the other side of the table. She looked at him from above the glasses which sat on her big nose and said, "Name".

"Adolph Sphitz".

"Hmph, is that with a 'Z'?"

Adolph nodded.

"Right. Arr here we are. Let me see. Have you had any success with the list of job vacancies we gave you?"

"Well, I was looking for a slightly better job, I got an 'A' level in art you know."

"Yes we know, but I'm afraid you won't be able to get a job at the moment, not a good one at least. All the good jobs we get go in a few hours time. That's just the situation."

"Well, what's the best job you got at the moment?"

"You can label baked bean cans at Tesco's."

"You must be joking ... but how much money do I get?"

"£19 a week."

"Nah, that's not good enough, I can't even get a pair of good jeans for that."

The lady paused and looked back into her file. She pulled out a card and read it. Then she looked up and said.

"Here's one more job you can try. It's a job as an assistant in a fishmongers."

"No way. I'm not gonna cut up stinking fish all day."

"The pay is £24 a week. That's very good for the job."

"Yeah, I suppose so. Give me the address and I'll go and have a look at that."

The lady filled out a sheet, then she stamped it and gave it to him. She also handed him a piece of paper with the address of the fishmonger's on it. Adolph took it and walked from the booth.

Adolph hopped off the bus and looked across the High Street. The fishmongers was across the street. It looked very smart and expensive from the outside. Adolph dodged the cars crawling along the street and pushed open the door. He walked to the end of the counter where a smart looking middle aged man was standing. The man was wearing a dark blue pin stripe suit and had a dignified expression on his face. His hair was sparse and most of it was a silvery grey colour. He looked up as Adolph walked over to him.

"Hullo, the Employment Exchange sent me down. They said I could get a job here."

Adolph pulled out the form and

handed it to the man.

"Well don't look at me, I'm only an assistant, you want to see the manager, I'll take you to his office."

The man frowned at Adolph's pink plastic jacket and led him to a door. He knocked and a deep voice told them to come in. They walked in and the man introduced the manager to Adolph.

"This youth has just been sent to us from the Employment Exchange. Here's a form he gave me."

"Okay, take a seat. You can leave now Johnson."

"Of course, Sir."

The man left the room and the manager turned to Adolph.

"Hullo, my names Mr. Docwaite. Have you had any previous experience at working in either a fishmongers or a butchers?"

"No, but I used to boil beetroot at a grocery store."

"Hum, well I'm not sure whether that's good enough. Does fish brain make you sick?"

"Not particularly."

"Well that's something, if you work here you'll be seeing an awful lot of them."

"Does that mean I've got a job then?"

"Yes, I think we'll take you on, but I think you should wear something a little more, er, conservative when you turn up for work. You can start next Monday. Come in at 8 a.m. you work until 6 p.m."

"What? That's ridiculous! How long's the lunch break?"

"Oh, that's half an hour."

Adolph was about to tell the manager where he could stick the job, but he checked himself, after all, he needed the money.

"Okay, I'll be in on Monday."

Adolph left the fishmonger's and

walked along the crowded High Street. The people walking along dodged him as if they didn't want to have any bodily or visual contact. Adolph sneered at them and carried on walking down the street. A policeman stared at him as he went past,

"Oink, Oink".

Adolph mumbled under his breath. The cop gave him a hard stare. Adolph shuffled on, a large smirk on his face.

4. the Family.

When Adolph got home that night he was surprised to see his father who usually worked nightshifts. Adolph's father sat in an easy chair in front of the television. The programme he was watching was a documentary about the origins of stamp collecting. Adolph saw the show and sneered in disgust,

"How could you watch that crap?"

His father looked up,

"Moderate your language young man, you haven't left home yet."

"I don't have to moderate my language, you old fart. Watch your shitty little documentary. An' I got news for you, I ain't sticking round here for much longer. I've got a job, I don't have to depend on you anymore, and I'm certainly not going to grovel to you."

"What you need is a good spanking. In my day people like you were put in the Army. You wouldn't be so smart after some good exercise and hard work. I want to talk to you about these records you play. They're filth, absolute dirt, I will not allow them in my house, I read about them in the News of the World."

"You believe the stuff that thing prints, you must be ill. I'm not throwing away my records, in fact I'm going to go and play them now, and tomorrow I'm leaving, I'm moving into a flat in Camden."

His father turned around in surprise then began shouting,

"I don't care, in fact, as far as I'm concerned you can leave right now."

"Well you're not going to get your way. I'm leaving tomorrow."

With this Adolph turned around, and stormed out of the door and into his own room. Presently the noise of the New Wave could be heard as he blasted himself with his favourite songs.

Adolph played his records nearly all night and it was only just as dawn broke that he finally put his last record away and climbed into bed.

It was midday when Adolph woke up. He yawned, stretched, and hopped out of bed. He pulled on some clothes and walked out into the kitchen. His mother was standing by the stove cooking the midday meal. Adolph looked at her,

"Can I have my breakfast. Bacon, eggs and toasted tomatoes ...please."

His mother looked up,

"Can't you get it yourself, I'm very busy."

Adolph sighed and pulled himself up out of his chair, he went to a cupboard and pulled out a frying pan. He put the pan on the stove, then he changed his mind,

"No, I think I'll go and eat out."

"Why don't you eat lunch with us, just this one last time, please."

"No."

His mother looked at him angrily,

"Why not, can't you even give us the courtesy of staying to say goodbye to your father?"

"Don't talk to me about courtesy. When were you ever nice to me? You were always going out and just leaving me by myself. Now I'm changing the tables around. I'm gonna go out and leave you."

Adolph stormed out of the room and began to throw his clothes into a couple of suitcases. He picked up his cases and his box of records and walked towards the front door. His mother was standing by the door; he could see she had been crying.

"Look, you don't have to have a fit just because I'm leaving, you know."

"It's just that you're our only son

and we've brought you up from a baby to a man, we're sad to see you go, even if you're not a shining example, we still love you."

With this she threw herself onto him and hugged him for what seemed an eternity. Adolph sighed and said,

"Well goodbye then, I'll miss your breakfasts."

He turned around and slowly walked down the corridor to the lifts. Adolph waited for one of the battered lifts to appear then stepped in and surveyed the bored looking people travelling with him. They looked totally blank. The only expression on the faces of most of them was disgust at Adolph and everything he represented. As the lift descended to the ground level, Adolph picked up his cases and stepped out into the entrance hall of the tower block. The small crowd of people stepped out behind him, but an old man dressed up in an old black suit with lots of medals came up to him.

"Bloody commie, you should be put in prison. You're a traitor to the Queen, that's what you are. Why don't you go and live somewhere where you can't corrupt today's youth?"

"Look mister, I am today's youth, and you're going to be hearing a lot more of us if you don't sit up and take notice. There's gonna be some changes in this country pretty soon, an' you better be prepared for it."

But the old man wasn't listening, he was going off the other way, muttering about kids. Adolph sighed, then walked down to the bus stop. After a few minutes of patient waiting, a 31 bus stopped and Adolph got on leaving his cases in the luggage compartment and sitting on a seat on the upper deck of the bus. The bus was quite full up, because it was Saturday afternoon and many people were going to the West End and local shopping districts. Eventually the conductor came up to Adolph,

"Fares please."

Adolph looked up from the window and offered the conductor his money.

"Five please."

"You're not a five. I'll chuck you off if you're not careful."

"I've got proof that I'm a half, d'wanna see my passport?"

The conductor was thoughtful. Adolph knew that there was no way for him to prove his own age, because he didn't even have a passport. The conductor gave him the benefit of the doubt,

"Is your passport in those cases downstairs?"

"Yeah, I'm going on holiday."

"Well, I'll give you a five then, I haven't got time to check."

The conductor handed him a ticket and Adolph felt very pleased with himself.

Soon Adolph arrived at the door of his new flat. It was a very small one, just a bedroom, kitchen and bathroom-toilet. Adolph liked it because the owner was a Punk so all the furniture and decorations were to his tastes. On one wall there was a huge line of graffiti done in fluorescent pink aerosol paint, it said "No Elvis, Beatles or Stones in 77". On the other side of the room was more paint, the whole of that wall was just splattered with paint, above this "Destroy" was written in big black letters. Adolph was sorry that he could only stay there for a while, because Tony, the owner, was in prison for beating up a National Front heavy.

In the corner was a sound system. Adolph walked over to it and thumbed through a pile of records, most of them were new wave, but there were some Rasta records. Adolph picked out Bob Marley and put it on. As the music blasted out of the speakers he made a cup of tea.

5. THE PARTY.

It was a large, shabby house, with crumbling stone and peeling paint. The paint was probably white originally but now it was a dirty grey, marred by pigeon droppings. The lower windows were covered over by corrugated iron. The house had been squatted for three years now. Adolph banged on the door. Soon he heard footsteps and the door was opened by a black punk.
"Hi man. Howdya do? Why don't you come in? Got any booze, girls, dope, safety pins?"

"Yeah, I got some wine, some vodka and some cow who I gave the address to, she'll be here soon."

"Right, man, come in an' enjoy the music."

As Adolph walked in the stereo was vomiting out the Clash and a few kids were pogoing down the stairs. There were some Teddy girls, some hippyish types and quite a few punks. Adolph wondered if the Teddy girl was there. He walked into a large room. The walls were bare and dirty, but a luxurious stereo was playing and a strobe light flashed on and off. Adolph looked around. He saw the usual collection of party goers, some people he didn't know and a few good friends. Adolph waved to his friends,

"Oy, Roy, Sid, Captain Vicious. "How's the party?"

"It's okay. Some of the birds are good for a screw. Arf, arf."

Captain Vicious laughed. Adolph was amazed. Captain Vicious had a really weird laugh; it was very simple but no one seemed able to imitate him.

Adolph walked up the stairs. He was holding a bottle of vodka in his hand and was beginning to feel the effects of the liquid. As he stumbled, he looked up and he saw a face through the haze. He recognised it, but he couldn't place the features, then it clicked in his dazed brain. The girl was the Ted who he'd seen on Shaftesbury Avenue. She was dressed in a really sexy boiler suit. Apparently she had changed her image. She had a short spiky hair cut with a safety pin through one ear. She wore an ordinary sleeper through her left ear. She was wearing pink plastic sandals with lurex purple socks. The boiler suit was green and had plenty of safety pins and tears in it. She looked down the stairs at Adolph, and slowly advanced to where he stood. Adolph wondered what to do next. How do you get off with someone you don't even know? Adolph coughed, blinked and looked up at her,

"Hi, haven't I seen you before? My name's Adolph."

"Hi, my name's Thelma. Yes we've caught a glimpse. I've been looking forward to seeing you again. Nice party, eh?"

"Er, why don't we go off and find somewhere a little more quiet?"

The girl giggled. She didn't really seem like the giggley type though. They walked up the stairs to a small landing. Only a few couples were on the landing, which was untouched by the noise and rowdiness of the party. Most of the couples were sitting in dark corners, but Adolph couldn't see what they were doing. Thelma sat down on some stairs leading up to the second floor, Adolph sat next to her. He desperately searched for something to say. At last he had some small conversation ready.

"The last time I saw you, you were with some heavy looking Teds, an' you were dressed up like some sort of Blackpool rocker, but you've changed your image. Why?"

Thelma looked up and sighed.

"Well, it gets a bit boring with the Teds. The music's pretty shitty, an' the get-ups even worse. The only reason I ever became a Ted was because of Ned. He was my boyfriend, but he was more a middle aged drunk really."

She sighed again.

The conversation died.

"I've never been screwed by a punk before, do you want to be the first one?" she said.

It took Adolph by surprise but he immediately agreed and they ran upstairs to an empty bedroom. Adolph pushed open the door and Thelma took the bottle of vodka from his hand. She took a long swig from it and handed him back the bottle. There was only a quarter of the bottle left. He finished it off and they both fell down onto a huge waterbed.

"Cor, I'm floating," she said.

By now Adolph was fumbling around trying to undo her boiler suit, there were so many zips he wasn't sure where he was. Thelma stood up impatiently and undid the suit then smartly hopped into bed. She turned to Adolph and in a melodramatic voice said,

"Be gentle with me, my dearest."

They both started roaring with laughter, but downstairs, no one had anything to laugh about.

A large group of Teds were standing in the center of the room where the main party was going on. Since they'd come in, a sort of hush had come over the proceedings. The leader, as always was Ned. He stepped towards the record player with a record in his hand. He flicked the needle across the surface of the record that was on, and a loud scratching noise came through the speakers.

A punk rushed forward,

"Oi, what d'ya think you're doing to my record, greaseball?"

Ned turned round angrily,

"If you don't piss off I'll scratch

you like I did the bloody record."

The punk knew he couldn't do anything against all the Teds, who were just standing waiting for a fight to happen. He backed away,

"You ain't seen the last of me."

He stormed out and Ned's record began. Soon the Teds were bopping and jiving everywhere. The other party guests stood around at the side of the room. None of them dared change the record, which had been played about four times in succession. Some punks moved into the middle of the room. There were about eight of them. They all looked very nasty. They wore special dog collars round their necks. Hanging from their faded leather jackets were chains and huge safety pins. One punk had a pin through his nose, ear and mouth. He had on about half of a T-shirt which was held together by little linked safety pins. Several of the punks were holding bottles in their hands.

"Oi, what about a bit of punk then?" snarled Captain Vicious. The Ted looked up. There was a glint in his eye, which was barely visible underneath a flash pair of shades.

"Piss off. G'wan, go suck a safety pin! Get lost. The sight of you is making me feel bad. I got this dull aching in my knife hand. The only way to lessen the pain is to stab something, smash its skull in and stomp all over its brain. Not a pretty sight, is it boys?"

Ned turned around and the other Teds agreed.

"Yer just tell 'im Ned boy."

Ned looked at Captain Vicious.

"To think that Thelma wanted to be scum like you. I always knew she was nuts. . . ."

With this last word Ned stopped. There was no music.

"Oi! Where's my record?"

A punk held a small record in his hand. He held it up in the air and dropped it onto the floor, it clattered on the hard wooden boards and the punk dug a heavy boot into it.

"Oh dear, I seem to have broken it."

The punk grinned maliciously, but before anything else happened, Ned leaped onto the punk and began to throttle him. The rest of the Teds attacked Captain Vicious and the other six punks. Before long there was a shambles in the room as the opposing parties fought it out. Soon the fight spilled onto the quiet street. Ned hurled the record smasher into the road. The kid sprang to his feet in no time and aimed a kick at Ned's groin. Ned was too slow and the punk got him where it hurt most. Ned fell to the ground. The punk kicked him again. This time Ned was ready. He grabbed the punk's foot and pulled his leg into the air.

At the same time he leapt up and pulled a long narrow object from his pocket. A button was pushed and an evil looking blade glinted in the moonlight.

"This is where you meet the great safety pin in the sky, punk".

He drove the knife into the punks arm. Blood poured out at an amazingly fast rate, but still the punk had some fight left in him. He lunged out at Ned and caught him in the nose with a bottle. The Ted's head fell back against the wall with a thud as blood emptied from Ned's nostrils.

"You bloody rat! You're gonna die for this".

With one last final swing, Ned pushed the knife into the punk's stomach. The punk fell forward, winded, with a large gash in his T-shirt . A red stain was quickly spreading. The punk had turned a ghostly white, and was now vomiting blood and cheap booze over the pavement. Ned kicked the body to the floor. Some punks were being chased down the street. A Ted lay in the gutter with a gaping wound in the side of his head. Captain Vicious sat on the ground nearby. Holding a hand over a wound in his arm, Ned looked at the punk. Neither of them were in condition for another fight.

"You'd better tell any jerk who tries to get off with Thelma, my old lady, that if I sees him around with her, he's gonna get a knife in the guts, like this rat!"

Ned kicked the unconscious figure. Police sirens could be heard in the distance. Ned looked up.

"If I weren't in a hurry I'd leave an address for the pigs, but I've gotta go."

Ned turned around and hurried off down the street. Captain Vicious picked himself up and staggered into the house.

Upstairs, in a cold, dark room Adolph and Thelma lay happily asleep in each other's arms.

6. A DAY ON THE TOWN.

The day was bright which was unusual, especially for North Kensington. Adolph was hot. He pulled the blankets from the bed and dropped them onto the floor. He got out of bed and staggered drowsily over to a wardrobe. He pulled open the door and took out a faded green boiler suit, some clean underpants, and gold lurex socks. Adolph put them on and walked over to a mirror in the corner. He pushed a 'sleeper' through his ear and attached a safety pin through his nose. It was an extra large nappy pin. Adolph ruffled his hair with a comb and went into the kitchen.
He opened a box of large white eggs and took two out. He unwrapped the bacon and placed three pieces under the grill. He turned the grill on and sat at the kitchen table. Today was every punk's big day. The Sex Pistols,

the Damned and the Clash were all doing a free gig at the Roxy from one o'clock 'til three. He was going to take Thelma to her first punk gig, but first he was going round to her house to collect her and take her to the Hard Rock Cafe for lunch. The sound of sizzling bacon roused Adolph from his thoughts and he broke the eggs into a warmed up frying pan. The sound of cooking soon filled the kitchen and before long he was tucking into breakfast.

Thelma lived in Islington, just off the Angel, a seedy place full of crumbling houses and decayed, seedy streets. Adolph felt at home there. He made a mental note to get a flat there, some day.

Thelma's house was on a neat little terrace off the Pentonville Road. Most of the houses were quite well kept. Adolph judged the street as being quite posh. He rang the bell. Adolph heard footsteps. He decided that he should try and disgust Thelma's parents just for a laugh. The door opened and a jolly, intelligent looking man who was quite tall, answered the door. He smiled at Adolph. Adolph cleared his throat and gobbed on the doorstep.

"Allo, is Thelma 'ere? Get a move on, can't wait all bloody day yer know."

The man smiled, apparently unperturbed by Adolph's act.

"Come in, Thelma's been expecting you. My name's Michael, you're Adolph I suppose."

"Yeah, that's right."

Michael led Adolph into the house, Adolph looked at the paintings on the black walls. Michael showed him into a room, then went out again. Adolph slumped down on a cushion on the floor. From outside the room he heard a call,

"Thelma, some snotty punk's here."

Adolph pretended not to hear the

remark; he looked around.

The room was a large one. Although it was centrally heated, there was a large ornate fireplace with some logs piled onto it at one end of the room. The floor was covered with Persian carpets and very large cushions covered in silk. There was a huge satin bedspread hanging from the ceiling. It was pinned to the ceiling in each corner and at the centre, so it almost had the appearance of a hammock. A crystal chandelier hung from the ceiling, through a hole in the bedspread, which was patterned in exotic Eastern colours. Blooming trendies, thought Adolph to himself. There were plenty of old twenties style chrome lamps all over the room. A gigantic hi-fi system sat on a specially built shelf, which could open and close so that the system could blend in with all the other weird styles of the room. Just then Thelma walked in. She was dressed in a pair of black cotton dungarees, and a blue, yellow and red pinstripe blazer. She was wearing pale blue lurex socks and black plastic sandals.

"Hi, my dad thinks you're a real mess. Are you ready to go?"

"Sure, let's move."

Adolph jumped up and grabbed Thelma by the hand, he led her into the hallway and they pushed the door open and stepped into the neat little terrace street. They walked round the corner to the Angel underground station and were soon on a train to Green Park, near the Hard Rock Café. The train ran noisily along the tunnel. Thelma looked across to Adolph,

"Where are you taking me after the Hard Rock?"

"It's a surprise. You'll find out soon. You'll like it though, it's just our style."

"C'mon punk. I wanna know," Thelma snarled, pretending to be tough.

"No, I'm not telling you, you'll find out when it happens. Here's our station."

The Hard Rock was crowded, even for lunchtime. There was plenty of noise as Dr Feelgood blasted through some strategically placed speakers. A thick layer of cigarette smoke was being wafted out of the cafe by large ceiling fans.

Adolph and Thelma finally left the queue and were beckoned through the maze of tables to the bustling crowd standing around the bar. Adolph slipped ten pence into the pinball machine while they waited to be seated and a ball bounced up in front of the springed cue. Adolph gently pulled back the handle and the spring bounced back into place, thrusting the heavy metal ball up the table and into the play area. It bounced between the pins, which lit up and flashed on and off occasionally.

Before long he had a few free

games on the clock, but Thelma nudged him and in an impatient voice said,

"Come on, let's get a table, and give me a drink. I'll have a Harvey Wallbanger."

"Okay then."

Adolph turned to the bar and called a good looking bargirl over to him.

"Give me a Harvey Wallbanger and a Tequila Sunrise please, and could you try and get us a table."

"Of course, just a minute."

The girl went and collected the two drinks. Soon she was back with them.

"There you are sir, that's two pounds please."

Adolph handed her the money.

"I'll see about your table now."

Within minutes Adolph and Thelma were seated at a small table in the corner of the cafe. They were on a low tier, and overlooked the rest of the clientele. Another pretty waitress came up with a menu,

"I'll just leave these with you."

She said, then moved off again. Soon Adolph ordered for them and he sat back in his chair.

"How do you afford these prices on the dole money you get?"

"Oh, I've got a job now, in a fishmongers."

"I wondered what the smell was."

"Very funny. It's quite well paid. It's a flash fishmongers you see. Anyway none of the money I get goes to anyone else so I have a lot of spending money on payday."

Adolph sat back even further in his chair and said in a mock aristocratic voice,

"Besides, someone of my calibre has to maintain standards, don't you know?"

The food arrived. Two platefulls of grease and hamburgers with a couple of Schlitzes to wash it all down. The couple tucked in hungrily. A long period of contented silence followed, interrupted only by belches from Adolph and deep, ecstatic moaning from Thelma.

"Cor, give me a plateful of grease and raw, half dead flesh anyday, an' I'll tear apart any canned vegetable eating pansy Popeye the sailor," Adolph boasted.

Then with one last flourish he popped a french fry into his mouth.

"Don't think I can manage a Cafe Hot Fudge Sundae, a dark delicious pool of Fudge at the bottom of a tall glass. A large scoop of banana ice cream floating in it, all this covered by a mountain of freshly whipped double cream lightly sprinkled with delicately chopped. . ."

"Stop. I can't take it anymore. I feel ill," groaned Thelma.

"Let's have a cup of coffee."

Adolph ordered the coffee and they talked over it until it was time to leave.

Eventually the underground train stopped at Covent Garden. Thelma and Adolph jumped onto the platform and ran upstairs

"C'mon, I still don't know where we're going."

"What's the time?"

Thelma looked down at her watch.

"Quarter to one."

"Just in time."

They stepped out of the station to the street and began to walk the route to the Roxy. Thelma had never made the journey there so she had no idea of where they were going. She was puzzled over this, so she would keep asking Adolph where they were going. Adolph would still not tell her though, and it was only when they arrived on the street that Adolph turned to her and said,

"Okay, we're almost there, I think I'll tell you where we're going now, it's the Roxy. Have you ever heard of the Roxy?"

"Yeah. Who are we going to see?"

"It's a special gig, to mark the anniversary of the Sex Pistols first ever gig. And they're got a couple of guest bands, the Damned and the Clash."

"Oh what? Really? I've always wanted to see them ever since I became a punk."

They arrived at the Roxy. A crowd of punks were standing around trying to impress each other when a door was opened by someone inside. Everyone suddenly turned around and there was a slow surge forward. The punks shuffled slowly up to the door, where a man sat collecting money for tickets.

There was another smaller crowd, more of a queue really, that was for people who already had tickets. A few stars were going through another door. This one didn't have a queue, but was used quite frequently. As the big names went in, Robert Plant and Mick Jagger were among them. Later on Keith Richard arrived, or Keef, as some of his fans know him. The crowd was not impressed by Mick Jagger, nor Keef, but did show slight welcome to Robert Plant who was almost a regular there.

Adolph and Thelma were soon in because they had tickets for the gig. Adolph had heard about the gig quite a while in advance so he bought tickets early.

Inside, a small room led to a corridor, which opened onto the actual stage and audience area. The crowd was in high spirits as they listened to the DJ's records, but they would not be satisfied until they got the goods from the Pistols, Damned and Clash. The couple moved through the crowd to the bar, which seemed to have an extended license. Once Adolph got to the bar, he turned to Thelma,

"What do yer want to drink?"

He was putting on his 'tough' voice.

"Well, I think I'll have a special brew."

Adolph ordered two large cans of special brew, then he changed it to four. Eventually they managed to get to a good place. They stood just to the side of the centre of the stage, so that they wouldn't get too crushed.

"I like to have room to pogo," Adolph said.

"Yeah, me too!" Thelma said.

The whole crowd seemed to grow bigger and bigger until the hall could no longer hold anyone else. There was a gallery higher above where Mick, Keef, and Robert held court over everyone else.

That's part of the rock scene. The good thing about being a rock legend is that people will always pay some attention to you, as well as idolize you sometimes.

There was a cheer from the crowd as the Damned walked on stage.

Brian James plugged in his guitar and Rat Scabies got behind his drum kit, Captain Sensible and Dave Vanian walked to the front with Brian. Captain Sensible spoke into the microphone.

"'Ello, we're glad to see you 'ere. D'wanna pogo? Well here's a song to do it to. New Rose:"

Rat pounded into a kettledrum and guitars sprang into action. The vocalist shouted,

"I gotta new rose. . ."

Then the rest of the band went at such a pace you could hardly keep with it. The band got through the song then wham, they stopped. Most of the crowd clapped enthusiastically and cheered encouragement. A lot were just too out of breath after a good shot of pogoing. The band went through their entire set, which seemed to be over in ten minutes.

The Clash came on next, the crowd gave a roar of appreciation as the band broke into their song,

"White riot
"I wanna riot
"White riot
"A riot of my own."

The song was over in minutes and the band spat on the audience as the small crowd crammed into the club punched the air with their fists. The next song was '1977'. The band played this extremely fast. The crowd at the front were pogoing about three feet into the air. Some punks were so enthusiastic that they jumped on each others' feet. A punk fell over, more fell on top of him and there was a small pile up at the front of the stage. Joe Strummer of the Clash picked up a cup of beer and threw it on to the crowd, the singer responded by shouting over the microphone,

"I''m hot. Cool me off".

The crowd at the front threw their cups at him, about eight pints of bitter and lager showered over the punk's head. The set continued, Adolph was pogoing all over the place, Thelma joined him and they bounced up and down until the end of the set. The Clash stood there on the tiny stage.

"Who want's an encore?"

"We do," chanted the crowd in unison.

"Well, 'ere ya are"

The band started playing and the words screamed through the P.A. at the front of the stage,

"Career opportunities
"the ones you never miss
"career opportunities are where
"they sling you out the door . . ."

At the end of the song the crowd surged forward as a natural impulse. The band walked off the microscopic stage.

A DJ put on a record. It was 'Peaches' by the Stranglers. The song was played until near the end, the vocals were sneered out and the crowd joined in,

"Oh no. I missed the Charabang,
I'm stuck here for the summer,
What a bummer
But I can think of a lot worse
places to be,
Like down in the street
Or down in the sewer.
Or even on the end of a skewer."

The crowd waited impatiently throughout the interval, but the Pistols were still not on stage. The crowd began to get restless and were soon chanting,

"Pistols, Pistols. We want the Pistols."

A few fights broke out at the back of the room. A person was trying to push his way through the crowd to the front. A punk turned around and snarled at him,

"Oi! Piss off. Right?"

"Nah! I'm trying to get through, so go suck a safety pin!"

The first punk turned around and drove a fist into the other's face. The man fell back in surprise, but balanced himself and aimed a vicious kick at his aggressor's groin.

"Why you little. . ."

But before the punk could finish his sentence a second kick hit him in the teeth. Blood and teeth ran from his mouth, but he struggled up again and butted into the man. They both fell back, knocking people out of the way. More punks turned around in anger as their beer and belongings were knocked from their hands. Soon there was a large bundle at the back of the room and as patience and tempers became more frayed, even more arguments broke out all over the club. After half an hour a man walked out on stage,

"Sorry we kept you waiting, now the birthday band themselves, the Sex Pistols!"

A roar of appreciation rose from the crowd and Johnny Rotten staggered to the front of the tiny stage. He was wearing a black torn boiler suit. Around his neck he wore a dog's collar, and his legs were joined by a chain about two feet long. In one hand he held a large can of lager.

He was bleary eyed and his fair hair was dark with sweat and grease.

" I don't know why you stupid snots waited, cause we ain't gonna play with all you morons fighting, now get up and move."

Johnny looked up at the balcony, he saw a few familiar faces in the audience up there.

"Wot's this. Old farts gathering day?"

Mick Jagger and the others of his entourage blushed a deep purple under their Californian suntans. Johnny Rotten turned and looked out into the crowd with his usual demented stare. He brushed some hair from his eye and said,

"The BBC won't play it, Woolworths won't stock it, but it ain't gonna stop you from buying it."

Then the Pistols blasted into 'God Save the Queen'. The song had everyone in the Roxy pogoing, and when it was finally finishing the crowd joined in with the chant of 'No future'.

Sid Vicious wiped his face with the sleeve of his leather jacket.

"If a Mr M. P. Jagger would like to meet me outside the Roxy later on, he might get a good kicking."

The band then continued with their set. They played all of their best songs, which included 'Anarchy in the UK' and 'Pretty Vacant'. When the Pistols' set finally finished, a happy crowd of punks left the Roxy.

Adolph and Thelma walked through the bright sunshine to Leicester Square.

As they walked, Adolph held his arm around Thelma. Unknown to them, a large draped figure was standing across the road watching. It was Thelma's old boyfriend, Ned, the Ted. Ned watched them and his eyes blazed with hatred. His fingers twitched around a flick knife in his pocket, but he knew that he couldn't kill Adolph there and then.

Adolph and Thelma stood on a crowded railway platform. A train eventually slowed to a halt and they hopped on as the doors slid shut, but before the train could move on again, the doors re-opened. Ned heaved them apart and stepped into the same carriage as Adolph and Thelma. He picked up an old newspaper and hid behind it as he waited for the two punks to get off the train.

At the door of her house, Thelma turned around and kissed Adolph, she had the key in the door and was just going to walk in when Adolph said,

"Let's go to Kings Road tomorrow."

"Okay, look I'll meet you here tomorrow at about one o'clock, see ya."

"Right, bye bye."

Adolph turned around and walked back down the street. A lone figure stepped from the shadows and slowly followed Adolph. Adolph turned into a deserted side street. The follower quickened his speed, then he shouted out.

"Oi you!"

Adolph spun round. It was Ned, the Ted. Adolph looked at him knowing why he was there, but he played for time,

"Whaddya want?"

"I want you, spiky top. An' you

know why, you been messing around wit' ma bird, ain't ya?"

"She isn't yours anymore, she doesn't wanna know you. She wants me, so there's no way you're gonna get her back."

Adolph turned to walk away.

"That's what you think buster."

Ned ran at Adolph and kicked him into the street, but Adolph was too agile. As he fell, he grabbed his huge loafer in his hand and pulled Ned down with him. Ned attacked him with even more fury than ever, and as he punched Adolph in the face, his left hand pulled out the lethal looking blade. Adolph looked up in surprise as the knife slashed within inches of his face, but his reactions were quick and he gave Ned a hefty kick in the groin, Ned gasped and fell forward, wounding himself on his knife. Adolph wiped blood from his face and was about to leave when Ned struggled back up. This time he seemed to fight with even more fury. He slashed the air around Adolph with the knife, but Adolph was always too quick for him. Ned soon began to tire and Adolph finally gave him one good punch in the face. Blood spurted out from the Ted's nose and he looked very surprised as he staggered, then fell to the ground. Adolph gave Ned one last kick, then picked up the knife and plunged it into the Ted's back. Ned twitched around on the floor until with a final struggle he lay still.

Adolph wiped the sweat from his face and put the knife away. He looked around. There was no one on the street. Adolph walked slowly down onto the main road and went into a public lavatory to clean himself up.

7. THE END.

Adolph hadn't slept well the night before, and he yawned as he walked on the street he'd killed Ned. Adolph didn't like going that way, but it was the shortest route to her house. As he walked up the street, a sign came into sight. It was a green police sign and had an appeal to witnesses to a murder. He shuddered as he walked past the sign, thinking that there might be someone watching him in a squad car. He decided that he wouldn't tell Thelma what had happened but as he got nearer to her house he began to get a feeling that she knew he'd murdered Ned.
Adolph rang the doorbell, Thelma answered. She seemed depressed.

"What's wrong with you? asked Adolph.

"Nothing. . . . well. . . . . er. . . .I'll tell you later."

She came out and they walked to the station together. They walked in silence until finally Thelma turned to Adolph.

"I read about Ned. You killed him didn't you? It must have been you. He was following us all the way home, did you know that?"

Adolph sighed,

"Yeah, it was me. I was just walking along the street when he came up to me. I told him you didn't wanna see him anymore and he attacked me when I walked away."

Thelma looked at him; there was a tear in her eye,

"Don't worry, I'll stand by you. Did anyone see the fight?"

"Nah, an' if they did they wouldn't wanna get involved."

Thelma and Adolph got off the train at Sloane Square and walked down Kings Road towards the Roebuck and the Man In the Moon. The Roebuck was one of Adolph's favourite pubs but the Man In the Moon had a lot of punk clientele.

It was bright Saturday afternoon. Kings Road was very crowded. By the time Adolph and Thelma got to the Kings Road Theatre, they were pretty tired. They'd seen a lot of Teds on the way but surprisingly they hadn't been beaten up yet. As they passed the theatre, a group of Teds across the street caught Adolph's eye.

"Hey, aren't those the Teds that Ned used to hang around with?"

Thelma looked at them,

"Yeah, but it'll be okay. I know them quite well. I don't think there'll be any trouble."

The two punks had caught the Teds eyes as well, and about eight Teds crossed the road. There were five Teddy girls as well. The Teds started to follow Adolph and Thelma. Soon they caught up with them. One of the Teds shouted out to Adolph.

"Oi, punk: I wanna word with you, what you doing down 'ere? Did I give you permission to walk on this street?"

"Nah, I don't need your permission, this is a free country."

The Ted glared and moved nearer Adolph.

"You being cheeky son?"

Before Adolph could answer, Thelma stepped forward,

"Hi Alf. Remember me? Ned's old girl. Well, Ned wouldn't like me to get hurt would he? He wouldn't want me to be upset would he?"

"Ned's dead," the Ted said sadly.

"Anyway 'e don't care about you. You're a traitor."

With these words the Ted slapped Thelma round the face. She fell back in surprise. Adolph furiously punched the Ted in the mouth, but before he could blink again, all the Teds set onto him. The five Teddy girls started beating up Thelma. She grabbed one of them by the hair and banged her head into a window, the glass shattered around the girl's head but Thelma had no chance against the other four girls. They soon formed a vicious circle round her and were battering her although she fought bravely. Adolph was doing no better. Eight Teds stood around him as he lay unconscious on the ground. A thin trickle of blood was running from his mouth. The fighting stopped. Thelma, bruised and cut, looked at Adolph, thinking he was dead. She pushed her way through the Teds and fell to her knees next to Adolph. She laid a hand on his forehead and laid her head on his chest to see if he was alive. He was. Thelma breathed a sigh of relief and knelt next to Adolph, waiting for him to wake. The Teds stood around. They were not sure what had happened.

"You've bloody killed 'im;" exclaimed one of them.

"Nah. He's alive, c'mon let's get out of 'ere before the cops get here."

The Teds turned and started to walk away, but one girl stayed behind. She watched Thelma as she kissed Adolph's forehead and face. Then all of a sudden she plunged forward. There was a flash of cold steel as a flick knife was embedded in Thelma's back. Thelma gurgled and fell over Adolph. The Teddy girl then plunged her knife into Adolph's neck. She struggled up to her feet.

"I killed two for you Ned!" the girl shouted. She ran down the street, pushing people out of the way.

A man rushed from the shocked crowd that stood watching the two dead bodies on the street.

"Quick! Don't just stand around, get an ambulance or something."

No one moved.

"God no wonder the country's gone

to the dog's:" the man shouted at them. The crowd just stood looking at Adolph and Thelma as they lay in a huge pool of blood, just watching as the sound of police sirens grew louder and louder.

The End.

Epilogue.

Apathy in the UK. An undercurrent of national dissatisfaction undermined the morale of 1970s Britain. Inertia and lethargy were setting in. No jobs, dole queues, no money, no girlfriend, no car. Unemployment was rife - and poverty, crime and violence had become more prevalent. The situation was set to worsen.

In the summer of 1976, at the dawn of the Punk explosion, West London's Notting Hill Carnival saw the first of a long series of street riots. (Jamaican history had been built on traditions of rebellion against oppressive state rule, and, now, a new generation were fighting back at the abuses of the system, police harassment and racial injustice). Notting Hill punk rock band The Clash yelled we want a riot of our own (a "White Riot") - and along came a warped looking nutter called Johhny Rotten screaming "Anarchy in the UK". Punk was born. It was an age of experimentalism, cultural re-evaluation - and as powerfully inspiring and strikingly "new" as the 60s Hippie Movement had been ten years before.

Ours was the punk generation. Wacky clothes mirrored the futility that we faced. Multicoloured hair-dos and fluorescent clothing blossomed like a rainbow in a grey sky, against a drab urban backdrop during the long cold wet winter of 77. In the King's Road there were clashes between Teddy Boys and hard-core Punk rockers. Graffiti and fly-posters (advertising records and gigs) splattered the walls of the inner cities. Punk songs became slogans and anthems to the degenerate generation.

Gideon was a local face, a real wisecracking smart Alec, who despite his youth, always seemed wiser than his years. Being cheeky - many, at times, found him obnoxious though no one ever held a lasting grudge. He had a sharp-witted tongue but a good heart and a keen wry sense of humour. His inimitable, 'audacious smiling style' brought laughter to many a pub, club, pool hall and street corner. He was a good hustler, a great buddy and we had much in common. We partied at the same local all night Reggae 'Shebeans' and dances. We were both caught in the thick of the '76 Notting Hill riots and shared the love of multi-racial culture. Though younger than me, he had bigger bags under his eyes as he usually burnt the candle at both ends. He thrived on backstreet excitement and urban danger was no stranger to him (I might have known he'd never make it to old age). He loved the nitty-gritty, was loaded with experience and totally immersed in street life. Gideon knew my band well, often playing washboard with the original line-up of my first group, Gaz's Rebel Blues Rockers, and cheerleaded audiences in the early days of the Trojans (watched often by Joe Strummer).

Gideon Sams epitomised the punk experience in this little book "The Punk", which was originally written as an English lesson project. (Gideon had been to ten different schools: Holland Park Comprehensive being the last, after a contretemps with the headmaster). The storyline for Gideon's book was set mainly in our area, London's W10, amidst such local landmarks as Trellick Towers and Portobello Road. It is a testament to the times, with people and places I will always remember with affection. Though fictitious, it reads typical of a genuine slice of our local history. I'm so glad that Gideon's book will ensure he'll be remembered by ever more people the world over. Nice one, Gideon.

Gary (Gaz) Mayall -

Founder of the legendary Gaz's Rockin' Blues (London's longest running club) and lead singer of The Trojans.